The Trow-Wife's Treasure

THE
Trow-Wife's
Treasure

OLIVIER DUNREA

FARRAR · STRAUS · GIROUX

WORD LIST

hoosie	*house*
Nord Eyris (nord aeris)	*"North Island"; mythical island off the northwest coast of Europe*
och	*exclamation of surprise, regret, or sorrow*
one year and a day	*one year, according to the old lunar-calendar reckoning using thirteen months in a year, with 28 days in each month, always having one day left over (28 x 13 = 364 + 1 = 365 days)*
puir	*poor*
thoo	*you*
thoo's	*your*
thooself	*yourself*
trow (trou or trau)	*"He who loves stone"; ancient race of troll-like creatures*
trow-bairn (trou-bearn)	*young or infant trow*
trow-wife	*female trow; usually older (as compared to a trow-maid)*
yon	*that*

The text of this book is set in Post Medieval Roman. The gouache paintings are rendered on Fabriano Ingres paper.

Copyright © 1998 by Olivier Dunrea. All rights reserved. Distributed in Canada by Douglas & McIntyre Ltd.
Color separations by Prestige Graphics. Printed in the United States of America by Berryville Graphics.
Designed by Lilian Rosenstreich. First edition, 1998

Library of Congress Cataloging-in-Publication Data
Dunrea, Olivier.
   The trow-wife's treasure / Olivier Dunrea. — 1st ed.
     p.   cm.
   Summary: On the mythical island Nord Eyris, a kind-hearted farmer goes to great lengths to help a mother troll find her missing "bairn."
   ISBN 0-374-37792-8
   [1. Fairy tales. 2. Trolls—Fiction.] I. Title.
PZ8.D965Tr   1998
[E]—dc20   96–24030

For Pam and Phil

On a small farm in Nord Eyris lived a farmer named Bracken Van Eyck and his dog, Caleb. He was not a wealthy farmer, but he was a generous one. He raised a small flock of chickens, six geese, several pigs, and one brown cow. In his fields he grew barley, onions, and potatoes.

Every day, Bracken tended to his animals. He worked in the fields. He played with Caleb and read his books. He helped his neighbors if they needed him.

One misty evening, as Bracken and Caleb walked toward the barn, the farmer saw a small, strange woman standing by the barn door. From her clothing, Bracken knew at once that she was a trow-wife.

"Good evenin', fellow," said the trow-wife, wringing her hands. "Can thoo no help me find me bairn? The tricksy wind swept 'im away an' he's lost somewhere hereabouts on thoo's farm."

"But of course I'll help you," replied Bracken. "Where did you last see your child?"

"The wind took 'im to yon wee hoosie," said the trow-wife, pointing to the henhouse.

"Let's begin looking there," said the farmer.

They quickly strode to the henhouse. Bracken opened the door and peered inside. He saw nothing but roosting hens. He looked in the nesting box outside the henhouse. He saw only an empty nest. There was no trow-bairn.

"He's not here," Bracken said to the trow-wife.

"Och, but thoo mus' git me bairn back to meself!" cried the trow-wife.

"Let's try the pighouse," the farmer said.

The trow-wife followed him across the barnyard to another small building. Bracken opened the door and went inside. He saw nothing but Brunhilde and her piglets, snoring softly in the straw. He looked in the feed box outside the pighouse. But all he saw was mash for the pigs. There was no trow-bairn.

"He's not here," said Bracken, shaking his head.

"Och, but thoo mus' git me bairn back to meself!" cried the trow-wife.

"We'll look in the barn," said the farmer.

The trow-wife trudged silently behind him. Bracken threw open the barn doors and stepped inside. He saw the geese huddled in their pen. He saw his cow contentedly chewing her cud. He searched everywhere. There was no trow-bairn.

The trow-wife did not come into the barn but stood at the door, peeking inside.

Just then a gust of wind blew through the barn. "Och, there goes me bairn!" cried the trow-wife.

Bracken looked up and caught a glimpse of a small green bundle tumbling through the air and out the window. "Come on!" he cried. "We shall get him back yet."

The farmer and the trow-wife ran across the stony downs, following the small green bundle.

"Och, me wee bairn!" cried the trow-wife.

The wind swept the baby onto the top of a standing stone.

"Can thoo no help git me bairn from yon stone?" cried the trow-wife.

"I'll do my best," said the farmer. He gripped the stone between his hands and legs and slowly inched his way toward the top, where the baby balanced.

As the farmer climbed, thick mists rose from the ground, hiding the trow-bairn. Below him, Bracken heard the trow-wife's thin voice.

"Ha' thoo no got hold of 'im yit?" she cried.

"I'm near the top of the stone, but I cannot see the baby," Bracken called down to her. He felt for the trow-bairn. His hands closed on empty air.

"Oo, the wind's taken 'im off agin!" cried the trow-wife. "Me bairn's goin' to be lost forever."

Bracken slid down the stone and ran after the
child. The trow-wife scurried close behind him.

The wind took the trow-bairn to the top of an
oak tree. The farmer and the trow-wife followed.
The wind took the trow-bairn to the top of an
ancient burial mound. The farmer and the trow-
wife followed. The wind swept the trow-bairn to
the top of the barn. The farmer and the trow-wife
ran after the blowing baby. Then the trow-bairn
disappeared!

"I think I know where he's gone," said the farmer. "He's not lost yet." Bracken ran into the barn and brought out a wooden ladder. He placed the ladder against the roof of the barn and quickly climbed up. His hands felt along the roof. Suddenly a hidden door sprang open. And there sat the trow-bairn safe and sound.

"I have found him!" shouted the farmer, quickly grasping the baby. Bracken held the trow-bairn tight and climbed slowly down the ladder to the trow-wife.

"Och, me wee bairn! Meself is glad to hold thoo onct agin."

Bracken watched happily as the trow-wife cradled her child.

"Listen, fellow," said the trow-wife gravely, "come thooself to the standing stone circle the morrow at dusk and meet meself onct more." Then the trow-wife slipped away and vanished from sight.

The next day, Bracken fed the hens and geese. He scrubbed the pigs and milked the cow. He worked most of the day in the fields. He played with Caleb. At the end of the day, he walked back to the farm. Slowly he passed the circle of standing stones. At the center of the circle, the farmer saw the trow-wife.

"Come, fellow," said the trow-wife. "Thoo mus' be rewarded for thoo's kind heart and willingness to help a stranger."

"I really need no reward—" Bracken began.

The trow-wife reached behind a stone and took out a small black hen. She stroked the hen gently and spoke quietly into her ear. Then she held out the hen to the farmer.

"Take this hen as me offering of gratitude for thoo's great kindness. Keep her well fed and warm for one year an' a day. Then thoo shall receive a trow-wife's treasure worth having."

The trow-wife handed the little hen to the astonished farmer. She stepped silently behind a standing stone and vanished. Bracken stared at the small hen. She looked quite ordinary.

For one year and a day, the farmer treated the little black hen with kindness. She seemed content, although she never laid any eggs.

At twilight at the end of the year and a day, the farmer tucked up the farm for the night. In the fading light, Bracken walked to the henhouse. Inside, the hens roosted and clucked softly to themselves. The trow-hen, as the farmer called the little black hen, sat in a nesting box. He thought this odd and lifted her out of the box.

Then in the straw Bracken saw a single golden egg! He stared at the egg. He lifted it and felt its warmth and weight. "It must be worth a fortune," he said to Caleb. "What am I to do with so much wealth?"

As the farmer and his dog walked back to the house, the trow-wife watched from the haystacks. She smiled. She knew what the farmer would do with his wealth. Then she slipped away into the night.

From that day on, Bracken Van Eyck was a wealthy man. The trow-hen continued to lay golden eggs, and the farmer continued to be kind and generous to friends and strangers alike. And for the remainder of his days, he kept the little trow-hen well fed and warm.

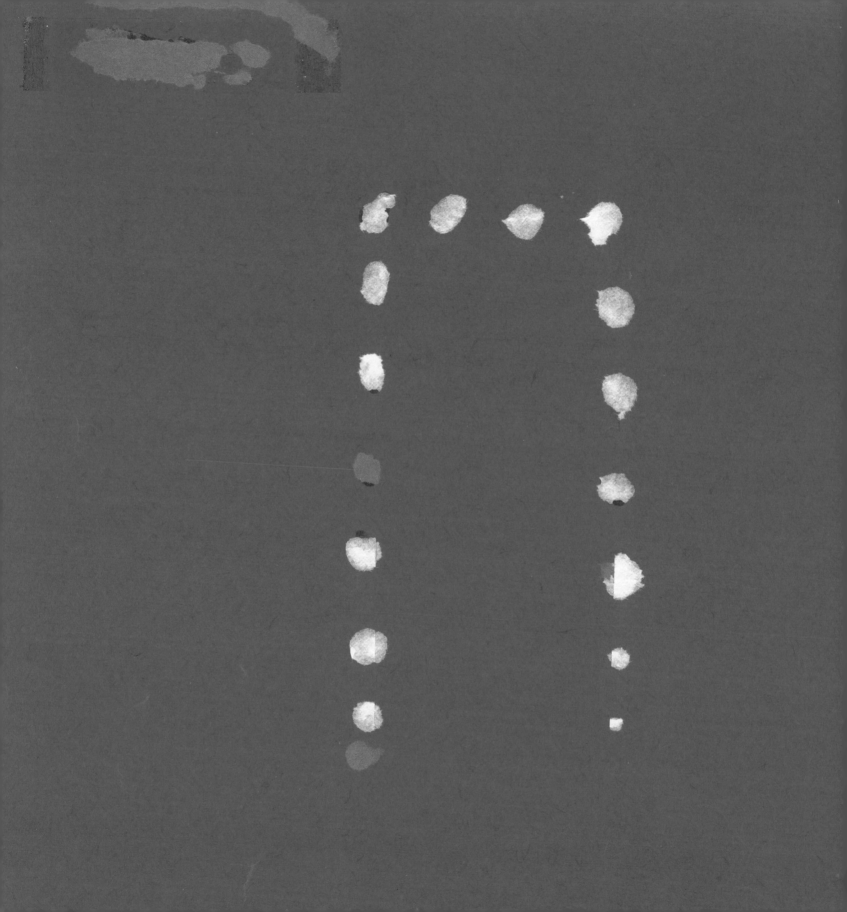